WINTER OLYMPIC SPORTS

FIGURE SKATING

by Joseph Gustaitis

Words that are defined in the glossary are in **bold** type the first time they appear in the text.

A table of abbreviations used for the names of countries appears on page 32.

Crabtree editor: Adrianna Morganelli
Proofreader: Crystal Sikkens
Editorial director: Kathy Middleton
**Production coordinator and
   prepress technician**: Katherine Berti
Developed for Crabtree Publishing Company by
RJF Publishing LLC (www.RJFpublishing.com)
Editor: Jacqueline Laks Gorman
Designer: Tammy West, Westgraphix LLC
Photo Researcher: Edward A. Thomas
Indexer: Nila Glikin

Photo Credits:
Associated Press: Wide World Photos: p. 14
Corbis: Bettmann: p. 9, 26, 27; Dimitri Iundt/TempSport: p. 13;
   Todd Korol/Reuters: p. 28
Getty Images: p. 8, 18, 24; AFP: p. 2, 4, 10, 12; Sports
   Illustrated: p. 6, 7, 16, 17, 21; Bob Thomas: p. 15, 22
Landov: Savintsev Fyodor/ITAR-TASS: p. 20; David
   Gray/Reuters: front cover
Wikipedia: Arnold C (Buchanan-Hermit): p. 29

Cover: Russia's Irina Slutskaya performs during her
free skating program at the 2006 Winter Olympics.

CONTENTS

Library and Archives Canada Cataloguing in Publication

Gustaitis, Joseph Alan, 1944-
    Figure skating / Joseph Gustaitis.

(Winter Olympic sports)
Includes index.
ISBN 978-0-7787-4022-3 (bound).--ISBN 978-0-7787-4041-4 (pbk.)

    1. Figure skating--Juvenile literature. 2. Winter Olympics--
Juvenile literature. I. Title. II. Series: Winter Olympic sports

GV850.4.G88 2009   j796.91'2   C2009-903212-0

Library of Congress Cataloging-in-Publication Data

Gustaitis, Joseph Alan, 1944-
    Figure skating / Joseph Gustaitis.
        p. cm. -- (Winter Olympic Sports)
    Includes index.
    ISBN 978-0-7787-4041-4 (pbk. : alk. paper)
    -- ISBN 978-0-7787-4022-3 (reinforced library binding : alk. paper)
    1. Figure skating. I. Title. II. Series.

GV850.4.G87 2009
796.91'2--dc22
                                              2009021492

Crabtree Publishing Company

www.crabtreebooks.com   1-800-387-7650

Published in Canada	**Published in the United States**	**Published in the United Kingdom**	**Published in Australia**
Crabtree Publishing	Crabtree Publishing	Crabtree Publishing	Crabtree Publishing
616 Welland Ave.	PMB16A	White Cross Mills	386 Mt. Alexander Rd.
St. Catharines, ON	350 Fifth Ave., Suite 3308	High Town, Lancaster	Ascot Vale (Melbourne)
L2M 5V6	New York, NY 10118	LA1 4XS	VIC 3032

FROM THE BEGINNING

Ice skates were not invented for fun, but for transportation. Today, figure skating is one of the most entertaining events in the Olympic Games!

THE FIRST SUPERSTAR

The first skating star was Jackson Haines (USA), who was born in 1840. At the time, figure skating was rather formal and movements were not flowing. Haines developed a new style of skating that was more graceful and dramatic. When he went to Europe to skate, he shocked everyone by skating to music!

Sasha Cohen (USA) performs at the 2006 Olympics.

ANCIENT ORIGINS

About 3,000 years ago, people in northern Europe invented skates to get across frozen lakes. The blades were made from animal bones. Iron blades were invented about 1,000 years later.

MODERN ICE SKATING

The sport of figure skating started in England in the 1800s, then it came to North America. Around the year 1850, a man named E. V. Bushnell invented a special steel skate that let skaters jump and **spin** in exciting ways.

FIRST WINTER WINNERS

At the first Winter Olympic Games in 1924, Gillis Grafström (SWE) won the men's gold medal in figure skating. Herma Planck-Szabo (AUT) won the women's competition. The winners in pairs were Helene Engelmann and Alfred Berger (AUT). There was no ice dance competition at the time.

OLYMPICS FACT FILE

- The Olympic Games were first held in Olympia, in ancient Greece, around 3,000 years ago. They took place every four years until they were abolished in 393 A.D. A Frenchman named Pierre Coubertin (1863–1937) revived the Games, and the first modern Olympics—which featured only summer sports—were held in Athens in 1896.

- The first Olympic Winter Games were held in 1924 in Chamonix, France. The Winter Games were then held every four years except in 1940 and 1944 (because of World War II), taking place in the same year as the Summer Games, until 1992.

- The International Olympic Committee decided to stage the Summer and Winter Games in different years, so there was only a two-year gap before the next Winter Games were held in 1994. They have been held every four years from that time.

- The symbol of the Olympic Games is five interlocking colored rings. Together, they represent the union of the five regions of the world— Africa, the Americas, Asia, Europe, and Oceania (Australia and the Pacific Islands)—as athletes come together to compete in the Games.

JUMPS AND OTHER MOVES

Jumps are the most exciting moves in figure skating. The best jumper often wins the competition. There are two basic kinds of jumps—**edge jumps** and **toe jumps**. Jumps can be done in combination, one after another.

NOT JUST JUMPS

A figure skating program involves more than just jumps. Other important elements are spins, **spirals**, and steps that connect the parts of the program together. These moves also show the skater's grace, flexibility, and skill.

Alexei Yagudin (RUS) executes one of the jumps that helped him win the 2002 Olympics.

ON THE EDGE

In edge jumps, the skater takes off from an edge of the skate. The three most common are the **Axel**, **Salchow**, and **loop**. The Axel is special because it's the only jump a skater does going forward. The skater winds up facing backward, so the Axel has an extra half turn in the air.

FROM THE TOE

In a toe jump, the skater uses the toe pick of one skate on takeoff. This helps the skater jump higher. Toe jumps include the **toe loop**, **flip**, and **Lutz**.

DOUBLES AND TRIPLES

If a skater spins once in the air after taking off, he's done a single jump. If he spins twice, it's a double jump, and if he spins three times, it's a triple jump. The triple Axel is 3 1/2 turns in the air. The first man to do one in competition was Vern Taylor (CAN) in 1978. Midori Ito (JPN) was the first woman to do one in competition, in 1989.

QUADS

A quad is a **quadruple** jump—four turns in the air! Kurt Browning (CAN) was the first skater to do a quad in competition, at the 1988 World Championships. Petr Barna (CZE) did the first quad in the Olympics in 1992.

IMPROPER BEHAVIOR?

Theresa Weld (USA) performed the first jump ever done by a woman in competition—a single Salchow, done at the 1920 Olympics. The judges scolded her for being "unladylike."

DID YOU KNOW?

Brian Orser (CAN) did the first triple Axel in the Olympics in 1984. Eight years later, Midori Ito (JPN) became the first woman to do the jump at the Olympics.

WHAT'S IN A NAME?

Some skating moves are named after the skaters who invented them or made them popular. One famous move is the Biellmann spin—named after Denise Biellmann (SUI)—in which the skater arches her back and holds one leg high above her head. (Men can do Biellmann spins if they're very flexible, but most of them aren't able to.)

OOPS!

Skaters can make mistakes when they jump. Some of the mistakes have special names. A "cheat" means the skater didn't fully turn in the air—for example, turning only two times instead of three when trying to perform a triple jump. A "waxel" is a failed attempt at an Axel jump. A "flutz" was supposed to be a Lutz jump, but the skater took off the wrong way, as if he was doing a flip jump instead of a Lutz.

THE OLYMPIC EVENTS

Women's singles, men's singles, pairs, and ice dance are the four figure skating events featured at the Olympics.

Scott Hamilton (USA) celebrates at the 1984 Winter Games.

SINGLES COMPETITION

The women's and men's competitions have two parts — the **short program** and the **free skating program** (or long program). Both are done to music. The short program lasts a maximum of two minutes and 50 seconds. A skater has to do eight required elements, such as jumps and spins. The free skate is four minutes long for women and 4 1/2 minutes long for men. It doesn't have all the required parts that the short program has.

SUPER STATS

A maximum of 30 women and 30 men participate in the Olympics in figure skating. The 24 women and men who do the best in the short program advance to the free program. A maximum of 20 pairs and 24 ice dance couples also participate. All of them advance to the last part of the competition.

DID YOU KNOW?

Athletes from Russia or the Soviet Union have won the most medals in Olympic figure skating, with 49. The United States is next, with 44.

PAIRS

Pairs skating is done by two skaters together. Each pair does a short program with required parts and a free skating program. The two skaters perform the same jumps and spins that singles skaters do, but they do them at the same time. Pairs also do special moves like **throw jumps** and overhead **lifts**.

ICE DANCE

Ice dance, which is done by two people, is like ballroom dancing on ice. The footwork is very difficult. Ice dance has three parts — the compulsory dance, the original dance, and the free dance.

BOOTS AND BLADES

Top figure skaters wear expensive skate boots that have been custom-made for them. The boots have thick, stiff leather interiors and added support around the ankles. The tongues have padding for flexibility. The blades, which have a slight curve, are specially sharpened. The width of the blade is about 0.15 inches to 0.25 inches (0.38 cm to 0.63 cm).

THE OLYMPIC RINK

In the 2010 Olympics in Vancouver, figure skating will take place at the Pacific Coliseum. The rink is 197 feet (60 meters) long and 98 feet (30 meters) wide.

A spin by Midori Ito (JPN) at the 1992 Games.

THE WOMEN

The women's singles is the most popular figure skating event at any Winter Olympics.

A FIRST FOR JAPAN

When Shizuka Arakawa (JPN) won the gold medal at the 2006 Olympics, she became the first Japanese figure skater to win Olympic gold. Arakawa had to come back from third place in the short program!

Beautiful moves helped Shizuka Arakawa (JPN) win the gold in 2006.

2006 OLYMPIC MEDALISTS: **GOLD: SHIZUKA ARAKAWA (JPN)**

SUPER STATS

The United States has won the gold medal in women's figure skating a record seven times.

DID YOU KNOW?

Women figure skaters used to wear heavy clothing and long skirts. Sonja Henie (NOR) was the first to wear knee-length skirts. Some judges did not like that.

THREE-PEAT

Sonja Henie (NOR) may have been the greatest woman figure skater ever. She is the only woman to win three Olympic gold medals in figure skating (1928, 1932, 1936). She also won ten World Championships! After the Olympics, she became a movie star.

FROM LAST TO FIRST

Sonja Henie (NOR) first appeared at the Olympics in 1924, when she was only 11 years old. She came in last! At the next Olympics, she rose to the top and came in first.

YOUNGEST AND OLDEST

The oldest woman to win an Olympic gold medal in figure skating was also the first — Madge Syers (GBR). She won in 1908 at the age of 27. In 1998, Tara Lipinski (USA) became the youngest winner. She was only 15! She is also the youngest person to win an individual event in Winter Olympic history.

LET'S DANCE

Many Olympic champions skate in ice shows after the Olympics. Kristi Yamaguchi (USA), the 1992 champion, starred in the Stars on Ice show. In 2008, she went on the TV show *Dancing With the Stars* and won first prize.

Sonja Henie (NOR), winner of three Olympic championships.

A LONG CAREER

Irina Slutskaya (RUS), the bronze medal winner at the 2006 Olympics, had a long and brilliant career. She competed at the World Championships for the first time in 1995 and won six medals — including two golds — over the next few years. She also won a silver medal at the 2002 Olympics. She retired from competition after 2006.

GREAT MOMENTS IN WOMEN'S FIGURE SKATING

Great performances, beautiful costumes, and upsets — that's why people watch women's figure skating!

Katarina Witt (GDR), in the performance that won her a second Olympic gold medal in 1988.

DUELING CARMENS

A funny thing happened in 1988 — two skaters chose the same music. They were Katarina Witt (GDR), who had won in 1984, and Debi Thomas (USA). The music was from the opera *Carmen*. Witt won the Olympic gold medal. Elizabeth Manley (CAN) finished second, and Thomas finished third.

COMEBACK

When Tenley Albright (USA) was 11, she came down with a case of polio, a serious disease that affects the muscles. She recovered and went on to become a top skater. She almost didn't win the Olympics in 1956, though. Two weeks before the Games, she hit a rut on the ice while practicing, and one of her skates cut through the other, slashing a blood vessel in her leg. Albright's father—a doctor—fixed her up, and she was off to the Olympics! There, she won the first-place votes of 10 of the 11 judges.

HARDING AND KERRIGAN

The showdown between two U.S. skaters at the 1994 Winter Olympics was one of the most watched TV shows ever. A month before the Olympics, an attacker clubbed Nancy Kerrigan on the knee. The ex-husband of skater Tonya Harding had hired the man so Kerrigan would not be able to skate in the Olympics. Kerrigan recovered in time and won the silver medal behind Oksana Baiul (UKR). Harding finished eighth.

DID YOU KNOW?

• Barbara Ann Scott was the first Canadian skater to win Olympic gold, in 1948. Tenley Albright was the first U.S. woman to win, in 1956. She later became a surgeon.

• Michelle Kwan's attempt in 2006 to win another Olympic medal failed because of injury. She got hurt while practicing for the Games and had to pull out. She was replaced by another skater—Emily Hughes (USA), the younger sister of 2002 winner Sarah Hughes, who wound up the competition in seventh place.

THE BIG UPSET

Few people thought Sarah Hughes (USA) would win the gold medal in 2002. The favorite was Michelle Kwan (USA), who was the World Champion. Things looked bad for Hughes going into the free skate. She was in fourth place, but she skated the best performance of her life and won the gold medal. Kwan wound up third. Kwan was one of the most popular figure skaters ever, but she never won an Olympic gold medal.

CLOSE COMPETITION

The 1980 Olympics featured one of the closest competitions ever in the women's event. Annett Pötzsch (GDR) and Linda Fratienne (USA) had both been World Champions in the years leading up to the Olympics. Both skated well at the Games, with Pötzsch winning the **figures** while Fratienne won the short program. In the end, Pötzsch skated away with the gold. Fratienne settled for silver.

THE MEN

In every Olympics, the men's singles competition keeps getting better, as the skaters perform fantastic feats.

A spectacular move by Evgeni Plushenko (RUS), the winner of the gold medal in 2006.

THREE-TIME WINNER

Only one man has won the Olympic gold medal in figure skating three times—Gillis Grafström (SWE). He won in 1920, 1924, and 1928, then he won silver in 1932. Grafström is also the only skater to win medals in four Olympics.

COMBO KING

Evgeni Plushenko (RUS) does amazing combinations of jumps. He was the first to do a "4–3–3" during a competition. In a 4–3–3, the skater does a quadruple jump, then two triple jumps—without stopping in between. No wonder Plushenko won the gold medal at the 2006 Olympics!

SUPER STATS

Male skaters from Russia or the Soviet Union have won the gold medal in every Olympics since 1992.

DID YOU KNOW?

When Ilia Kulik (RUS) won Olympic gold in 1998, it was the first time he was in the Olympics. The last man to do that was Dick Button (USA) in 1948.

THE BALLET DANCER

When John Curry (GBR) was young, he wanted to be a ballet dancer. His father wanted him to go into sports, and Curry chose skating. Curry combined great jumps with great art. He won the gold medal in 1976.

STILL FAMOUS

It has been more than 50 years since Dick Button (USA) won his second gold medal, but he might still be the most famous male figure skater. Button was not afraid to try really hard jumps during a competition. He was the first skater to do a double Axel (when he won in 1948) and a triple jump (when he won in 1952). After that, he became a TV announcer.

YOU CAN'T DO THAT AGAIN

Terry Kubicka (USA) did the only legal back flip ever in Olympic history in 1976. After the Games, the move was ruled illegal. Skating officials said that since the back flip is landed on two feet instead of one, it's not a "real" jump. The back flip may also be considered too dangerous. Kubicka came in seventh, and the back flip became a popular move in skating shows.

Elvis Stojko, one of Canada's finest, won two silver medals in the Olympics.

GREAT MOMENTS IN MEN'S FIGURE SKATING

Some of the most exciting athletes in Olympic history have been male figure skaters.

THE BATTLE OF THE BRIANS

Brian Boitano (USA) and Brian Orser (CAN) will always be connected. They skated against each other for years. One would win, and then the other. Everybody was excited when they met in the Olympics in 1988. In the free skate, Boitano skated first and delivered one of the best performances in Olympic history. Orser did almost as well, but he made a few little mistakes. Boitano won gold, and Orser won silver.

RUNNERS-UP

No Canadian man has ever won the Olympic figure skating championship, but some have come close. Brian Orser won silver medals in 1984 and 1988. Elvis Stojko won silver medals in 1994 and 1998. Stojko was a great jumper who studied martial arts. He was the favorite in 1998, but he had a painful injury and could not do his best jumps.

OH, BROTHER!

In 1956, Hayes Alan Jenkins (USA) won the gold medal and his brother, David, won bronze. Four years later, David won the gold, too!

FAST LEARNER

Evgeni Plushenko (RUS), the 2006 winner, could do all the triple jumps by the time he was 11 years old.

BEATING THE ODDS

Scott Hamilton (USA), the 1984 champion, is one of the world's most popular skaters. When he was a little boy, he had a disease that stopped him from growing. He wound up being only about 5'3" (1.6 m) tall.

Brian Orser (CAN) won silver medals in 1984 and 1988.

YOU MUST REMEMBER THIS

Sometimes a figure skater gives a special performance but doesn't win a medal. That's what happened at the 1994 Games to Kurt Browning (CAN). Browning was way behind in the standings after falling in the short program. In his free skate, he dressed up like the character played by actor Humphrey Bogart in the classic movie *Casablanca*. He also skated to music from the movie. Browning finished fifth, but he changed figure skating by adding a special dose of show business.

QUADS ALL OVER

The 2002 Olympics featured some of the most amazing skating ever in the men's long program. The three men's medalists— Alexei Yagudin (RUS), Evgeni Plushenko (RUS), and Timothy Goebel (USA)— each did two quadruple jumps in the free program!

THE PAIRS

Tatiana Totmianina and Maxim Marinin (RUS) perform a **death spiral** at the 2006 Olympics.

Pairs skaters—a man and a woman on the ice side by side—must perform difficult moves together with perfect timing and skill.

LEARN THE LINGO

Here are some pairs skating moves:

Spins—Skaters do some spins side by side. They also do "pair spins," where they hold each other.

Lifts—During a lift, the man holds the woman in the air. Sometimes she changes position during the lift.

Throw jumps—In a throw jump, the man launches the woman into one of the jumps that are done in singles skating.

Death spiral—In this scary-sounding move, the man turns while holding the woman's hand. She stretches out, almost lying on the ice, and goes in a circle around him.

OOPS!

Pairs skating can be dangerous. The woman can fall during a lift. In 2004, Tatiana Totmianina and Maxim Marinin (RUS) were skating in Pittsburgh. He lifted her into the air, but he tripped and she fell. She crashed onto the ice and had to go to the hospital. The pair did not compete for a while, but they came back to win the Olympics in 2006!

DID YOU KNOW?

Pairs from China wound up in second, third, and fourth place in the 2006 Olympics.

CHANGING PARTNERS

Pairs skaters don't always stay with the same partner. Irina Rodnina (URS) won the gold medal in 1972 skating with Aleksey Ulanov. Ulanov fell in love with a different skater, so Rodnina came to the 1976 Olympics with a new partner—her new husband, Aleksandr Zaytsev. They won in both 1976 and 1980.

Zhang Dan and Zhang Hao (CHN) in action in 2006.

SPECTACULAR FALL

During the free skate at the 2006 Olympics, Zhang Dan and Zhang Hao (CHN) attempted a very difficult move—a throw quadruple Salchow, which no pair had ever done successfully in competition before. She fell, though, and hurt her knee badly. The music stopped, and officials made sure she could skate. After a delay, the pair was able to continue. The crowd stood and applauded when they were done. Zhang and Zhang won the silver medal.

IN THE MIRROR

A man and woman in a pair usually jump and spin in the same direction, either to the left or to the right. Sometimes, though, the two people in a pair jump and spin in opposite directions. This is called mirror skating. One successful pair who did mirror skating were Jill Watson and Peter Oppegard (USA), who won the bronze medal in 1988.

PAIRS: JUDGES, JUMPS, AND ROMANCE

Pairs have been involved in some of the most dramatic moments in Olympic figure skating.

Both the Russian and Canadian pairs were awarded gold medals in 2002.

THE GREAT JUDGING SCANDAL

After the short program at the 2002 Olympics, Elena Berezhnaya and Anton Sikharulidze (RUS) were in first place. Jamie Salé and David Pelletier (CAN) were in second. Both teams skated well in the free skate, but the Russians made one small mistake. The Canadians were perfect. Many people thought they had won, but the judges gave the gold medal to the Russians. Later, one of the judges said she had been "pressured" to vote for the Russians. Olympic officials decided to give a second gold medal to Salé and Pelletier.

ROMANCE ON ICE

Sometimes pairs skaters fall in love and get married. Ludovika and Walter Jakobsson (FIN) were the first husband and wife team to win a gold medal, in 1920. Andrée and Pierre Brunet (FRA) won the gold medal twice, in 1928 and 1932. So did another married couple, Lyudmilla Belousova and Oleg Protopopov (URS), in 1964 and 1968.

THE SADDEST THING

Ekaterina Gordeeva and Sergei Grinkov (URS) won the gold medal in 1988. Three years later, they got married. In 1994, they won the gold medal again. But in 1995, Grinkov had a heart attack and died. It was one of the saddest things that ever happened in figure skating.

TURNING OVER A NEW LEAF

Artur Dmitriev and Natalia Mishkutenok (RUS) won the gold medal in pairs at the 1992 Olympics, then the silver medal in 1994. She decided to retire, but he wanted to continue skating. He found a new partner, Oksana Kazakova, and they won the gold medal in 1998. He became the first man ever to win the pairs competition at the Olympics with different partners.

FAMILY TIES

Sometimes pairs skaters are brother and sister. Kitty and Peter Carruthers (USA) were adopted when they were little children. At the 1984 Olympics, they won the silver medal.

TOO BAD

In 1980, skating fans were looking forward to a great Olympic contest, but it never happened. Irina Rodnina and Aleksandr Zaytsev (URS) were World Champions from 1973 to 1978. They took a year off in 1979 when Rodnina had a baby. That year, Tai Babilonia and Randy Gardner (USA) became World Champions. Which pair would win the Olympics in 1980? Unfortunately, Gardner got hurt, and he and Babilonia had to pull out of the competition.

ICE DANCE

A marvelous move by ice dancers Tatiana Navka and Roman Kostomarov (RUS).

Ice dance is somewhat like pairs skating, since a man and woman skate together to music. But in many ways, ice dance is very different.

A BRIEF HISTORY

Ice dance began in the last half of the 1800s. After skater Jackson Haines went to Europe, ice dance began to catch on. It was very popular in Vienna, Austria. There, dancers did the waltz on ice. Soon, waltzing on ice was popular in other countries. Other dances were also done on the ice. A book published in 1892 showed 17 different ice dances!

LEARN THE LINGO

Here are the three parts of ice dance competition:

Compulsory dance—All the couples do the same steps to a specific type of music.

Original dance—The skaters can choose the music, but everyone's music must be to a particular rhythm.

Free dance—This part has the fewest rules. The skaters can choose the music and the theme and can use unusual and difficult positions.

A LOT OF DANCES

The **International Skating Union** (ISU) announces what compulsory dances couples will do each year. Ice dancers have to learn a lot of dances! Some of them are the Argentine Tango, Blues, Cha Cha Congelado, Foxtrot, Paso Doble, and Yankee Polka.

GETTING DIZZY

Twizzles—turns done on one foot—are required moves in ice dance programs. Skaters usually do at least four turns during a twizzle.

Tanith Belbin and Benjamin Agosto gave the United States its first medal in ice dance in 30 years.

WHAT'S DIFFERENT ABOUT DANCE?

Ice dance doesn't have jumps. Lifts are done, but rules carefully spell out how high the woman can be raised. The skaters must also be close together and hold each other for much of the program. Lyrics are allowed in ice dance music—but not for other types of figure skating!

THE GREAT DANCERS

The magnificent Jayne Torvill and Christopher Dean (GBR) during the 1984 Olympics.

It takes a special twosome of skaters to win an ice dance competition. The Olympics have seen quite a few.

Couples from Russia or the Soviet Union have won seven of the nine gold medals ever awarded in ice dance. They have won 16 of the 27 medals overall.

DID YOU KNOW?

Tatiana Navka (RUS), who won the gold in ice dance in 2006 with her partner, Roman Kostomarov, is married to Aleksandr Zhulin, who won Olympic medals in 1992 and 1994 with his partner, Maia Usova. Zhulin is also Navka's coach!

THE FIRST OLYMPIC COMPETITION

When ice dance first appeared in the Olympics in 1976, Lyudmila Pakhomova and Aleksandr Gorshkov (URS) won the first gold medal. It was only a year after Gorshkov had a serious lung operation. Colleen O'Connor and Jim Millins (USA) won the bronze medal. The United States did not win another Olympic medal in ice dance for 30 years, until Tanith Belbin and Benjamin Agosto took silver in 2006.

THE BEST

Most people think that the best ice dance team ever was Jayne Torvill and Christopher Dean (GBR). They created a new style that changed ice dance forever. Once, they skated to music from a Broadway show and acted out the characters. Sometimes they used rock and roll, and other times they used Spanish music. After their free dance at the 1984 Olympics, the judges gave them 12 perfect scores! Ten years later, they returned to the Olympics and finished third. He was 35 years old, and she was 36.

TWO-TIME WINNERS

Only one couple has won the Olympic gold medal in ice dance twice—Oksana Grishuk and Evgeny Platov (RUS). They won in 1994 and 1998. One of the teams they beat in 1994 was Torvill and Dean.

GOLD AT LAST

Marina Klimova and Sergei Ponomarenko (URS) worked their way up the ranks. They won a bronze medal in 1984, a silver medal in 1988, and finally a gold medal in 1992. They are the only figure skaters to win three medals of different colors in the Olympics. They also won eight World Championship medals, including three golds.

CHEERS AND BOOS

The crowd was not happy with the results of the ice dance competition at the 1980 Winter Olympics. The gold medal winners, Natalia Linichuk and Gennadi Karponossov (URS), were formal, traditional ice dancers. The audience preferred the silver medal winners, Krisztina Regöczy and Andras Sallay (HUN), who skated in a more lively, upbeat style.

JUDGING

In many sports, it's easy to see who's the best. It's the person who swims fastest or jumps highest. But how do you know who's the best in figure skating?

The judges watching Jeffrey Buttle (CAN) at the 2006 Games.

WAITING FOR THE SCORES

At competitions, skaters and their coaches wait for the scores to be announced in an area near the ice called the "Kiss and Cry." That's because they'll be happy if the scores are good but sad if the scores are bad.

FIGURE SKATING JUDGES

The panel of judges who score each figure skating program have a difficult job, since it's hard to vote against a skater from your own country. The ISU makes the rules for judging international competitions. After the judging trouble at the 2002 Olympics, when one judge said she was pressured to vote a certain way, the ISU decided to set up a new judging system.

THE OLD SYSTEM

In the old system, each judge gave two marks. The first—for technical merit—judged things like how difficult the jumps were. The second mark—for presentation—judged the skater's style and how well she performed. Judges gave marks up to 6.0. A mark of 6.0 was "perfect."

THE NEW SYSTEM

The new judging system is much more complicated. Judges give two marks. The first mark—for technical elements—refers to the different moves a skater does. Every jump and every spin has a value assigned to it. Points are also added or taken away for how well or how poorly a move was done. The second mark—for program components—refers to the overall presentation of the program. The marks are added up for the skater's total score.

DIFFERENT MARKS FOR DIFFERENT MOVES

The harder the move, the more it's worth. A triple Axel has a base value of 8.2 points, while a double Axel is worth only 3.5 points. A triple Lutz has a base value of 6 points. Quadruple jumps are worth much more. A quadruple top loop has a base value of 9.8 points, and a quadruple Salchow has a value of 10.3 points. Some skaters think that quads are so hard that they should be worth even more!

WHAT ARE FIGURES?

Did you ever wonder why figure skating is called "figure" skating?

Janet Lynn (USA) did not win the Olympics because she did poorly in figures.

FIGURES AT THE OLYMPICS

Doing figures was a major part of early Olympic competition. In fact, at the first Olympic figure skating competition in 1908, "Special Figures" was a separate event. The gold medal winner was Nicolai Panin (RUS).

FANCY PATTERNS

Long ago, skaters saw that their sharp skate blades could cut lines into the ice. At first, they did simple patterns like a circle or a figure 8. Then they learned to do harder patterns. These patterns were called figures. Figures had fancy names like "the flying Mercury" and "the shamrock."

THE END OF FIGURES

In the early 1970s, figures were worth 60% of a skater's total score. The free skate was worth only 40%. The ISU decided to lower the value of figures and add the short program, beginning with the 1976 Olympics. Eventually, the figures were dropped entirely. The first Olympics without figures were in 1992.

Scott Hamilton (USA) tracing a figure.

BECAUSE OF FIGURES ...

Sometimes a great skater did not win a gold medal because of the figures. In the 1970s, Janet Lynn (USA) was one of the best and most popular skaters in the world. But at the 1972 Olympics, Trixi Schuba (AUT) was so good at figures that she won the gold. Lynn won the free program but wound up with the bronze.

EXAMINING THE ICE

After a competitor finished skating a figure, the judges would come out on the ice to examine the tracing. They would look closely at the figure, even getting down on their hands and knees to get a really close view. They looked to see if the circles were perfectly round and if all the circles were the same size. They also checked to make sure the skating edges were smooth.

CUTTING THE ICE

Jeannette Altwegg (GBR), who won the gold medal in 1952, was famous for her figures. When she skated one particular figure, she skated two circles, one on top of the other. A reporter said that it looked like she had "cut the ice only once."

A SNAPSHOT OF THE VANCOUVER 2010 WINTER OLYMPICS

FIGURE SKATING
THE ATHLETES

Everyone is getting ready for Vancouver in 2010! Olympic teams are still being determined. The listings below include the top finishers in a selection of events from the 2009 World Figure Skating Championships. Who among them will be the athletes to watch in the Vancouver Winter Olympics? Visit the Web site www.vancouver2010.com for more information about the upcoming competitions.

FIGURE SKATING EVENTS

Men—free skate:
1. Evan Lysacek (USA)
2. Patrick Chan (CAN)
3. Brian Joubert (FRA)
4. Tomas Verner (CZE)
5. Samuel Contesti (ITA)

Women—free skate:
1. Kim Yu-Na (KOR)
2. Miki Ando (JPN)
3. Joannie Rochette (CAN)
4. Mao Asada (JPN)
5. Rachel Flat (USA)

Pairs—free skate:
1. Aliona Savchenko/ Robin Szolkowy (GER)
2. Zhang Dan/ Zhang Hao (CHN)
3. Yuko Kavaguti/ Alexander Smirnov (RUS)
4. Pang Qing/ Tong Jian (CHN)
5. Tatiana Volosozhar/ Stanislav Morozov (UKR)

Evan Lysacek (USA) performs his men's short program, during the Torino 2006 Figure Skating competition.

Ice dancing—original dance:
1. Tanith Belbin/Benjamin Agosto (USA)
2. Oksana Domnina/Maxim Shabalin (RUS)
3. Meryl Davis/Charlie White (USA)
4. Nathalie Pechalat/Fabian Bourzat (FRA)
5. Jana Khokhlova/Sergei Novitski (RUS)

Ice dancing—free dance:
1. Oksana Domnina/Maxim Shabalin (RUS)
2. Tanith Belbin/Benjamin Agosto (USA)
3. Meryl Davis/Charlie White (USA)
4. Tessa Virtue/Scott Moir (CAN)
5. Nathalie Pechalat/Fabian Bourzat (FRA)

Tessa Virtue and Scott Moir of Canada perform their gold medal routine in the senior dance free program at the 2009 Canadian Figure Skating Championships.

THE VENUE IN VANCOUVER
PACIFIC COLISEUM

- **venue capacity: 14,239**
- **located in Vancouver, British Columbia**
- **elevation: 85 feet (26 m)**

GLOSSARY

Axel An edge jump in which the skater takes off from the forward outside edge of one foot and lands on the back outside edge of the other foot; the only jump a skater does going forward

death spiral In pairs skating, a move in which the woman stretches out horizontal to the ice while holding the man's hand as he turns

edge jump A jump in which the skater takes off from an edge of the skate

figures Formerly a part of figure skating competitions in which skaters were required to trace certain patterns on the ice

flip A toe jump in which the skater skates backward on a back inside edge, picks with the toe of one skate, makes a turn, and lands on the back outside edge of the other foot

free skating program The second part in singles and pairs competitions; sometimes called the long program

International Skating Union The ISU, the international governing body of both figure skating and speed skating

lift In pairs skating, a move in which the man holds the woman in the air

loop An edge jump in which the skater takes off from a back outside edge, turns in the air, and lands backward on the same edge

Lutz A toe jump in which the skater takes off from a back outside edge and lands on the back outside edge of the other foot

quadruple A jump in which the skater turns four times in the air; also known as a quad

Salchow An edge jump in which the skater takes off from a back inside edge, turns, and lands on the back outside edge of the opposite foot

short program The first part of singles and pairs competitions containing certain required elements

spin A move in which the skater spins on the ice like a top

spiral A move in which the skater glides across the ice with the non-skating leg extended into the air

throw jump In pairs skating, a move in which the woman does a jump after the man throws her into the air

toe jump A jump in which the skater is assisted by using the toe pick on one skate

toe loop A toe jump in which the skater takes off and lands on the same outside edge

FIND OUT MORE

BOOKS

Browning, Kurt. *A is for Axel: An Ice Skating Alphabet* (Farmington Hills, MI: Sleeping Bear Press, 2005)

Buckley, James. *Ice Skating Stars* (New York: DK Children, 2004)

Helmer, Diana Star, and Thomas S. Owens. *The History of Figure Skating* (New York: Rosen Publishing Group, 2005)

Jones, Jen. *Figure Skating for Fun!* (Minneapolis: Compass Point Books, 2006)

Milton, Steve. *Figure Skating Today: The Next Wave of Stars* (Richmond Hill, Ontario: Firefly Books, 2007)

Samuels, Rikki. *Kids' Book of Figure Skating: Skills, Strategies, and Techniques* (New York: Citadel Press Books, 2004)

Schwartz, Heather E. *Girls' Figure Skating: Ruling the Rink* (Mankato, MN: Capstone Press, 2007)

Thomas, Keltie. *How Figure Skating Works* (Toronto: Maple Tree Press, 2009)

WEB SITES

Skate Canada   www.skatecanada.ca
The Web site of Skate Canada, the national governing body of figure skating in Canada.

Canadian Olympic Committee   www.olympic.ca
The official site of the Canadian Olympic Committee, with information on athletes, sports, and the Olympics.

Golden Skate   www.goldenskate.com
A site that has news, articles, competition results, and other information about figure skating.

International Olympic Committee   www.olympic.org
The official site of the International Olympic Committee, with information on all Olympic sports.

International Skating Union   www.isu.org
The official site of the world governing body of skating.

Skateweb   www.frogsonice.com/skateweb
A Web site with links to all sorts of information about figure skating.

U.S. Figure Skating   www.usfigureskating.org
The Web site of U.S. Figure Skating, the national governing body of figure skating in the United States.

U.S. Olympic Committee   www.usoc.org/
The official site of the U.S. Olympic Committee, with information on athletes, sports, and the Olympics.

INDEX

COUNTRY ABBREVIATIONS

AUT — Austria
CAN — Canada
CHN — China
CZE — Czechoslovakia/Czech Republic
FIN — Finland
FRA — France
GBR — Great Britain
GDR — East Germany (1949–1990)
HUN — Hungary
JPN — Japan
NOR — Norway
RUS — Russia
SUI — Switzerland
SWE — Sweden
UKR — Ukraine
URS — Soviet Union (1922–1992)
USA — United States of America

Printed in the U.S.A. — CG

HISTORICAL NOTE: The Battle of Long Island was George Washington's first battle in the American War for Independence. It was a defeat. From Brooklyn, General Washington retreated to Manhattan, then to New Jersey, and in the last month of 1776, he crossed the Delaware River into Pennsylvania. Thus ended one of the longer and more bitter retreats in American history. On the day after Christmas, Washington crossed the icy Delaware once more into New Jersey. There, at Trenton and again at Princeton, his soldiers (many of whom had escaped from Brooklyn) defeated their enemy. In 1781, General Cornwallis finally surrendered at Yorktown. The British troops who fired on Samuel at Gowanus Creek on August 27th, 1776, were commanded by General Cornwallis.

Major Mordecai Gist led the Maryland state troops in the Battle of Long Island. He and Isaac van Ditmas are historical figures (although the arrest of van Ditmas did not actually occur). Samuel Abraham and Sana Williams are fictional, but modeled on the many nameless people of Brooklyn, slave and free, who made Washington's escape possible.

We stumbled ashore on Manhattan Island, where kind people wrapped us in blankets. They were smiling—the rope was across! The boats full of Washington's soldiers would follow. We had done it, together.

All through the night Washington's men followed that rope, boat after boat, across the water. In the stormy darkness, every soldier escaped from Long Island.

And so the fight for freedom would go on. It would take many long years before we would beat the British king, but never again did I wonder what freedom was, or what it cost. It was people pulling together. It was strong hands helping. It was one person caring about another.

And where was Washington? Many times that night Sana and I hoped to see him.

"Why, Samuel," Major Gist told us later, "he was that officer in the blue coat who asked you how deep the water was between Brooklyn and Manhattan. Last night the general arrested a farmer in Brooklyn for helping the British. That farmer, Isaac van Ditmas, turned all of his property over to the Army of the Continental Congress in exchange for his freedom. It seems now that you and Sana have no master."

From that day forward, we and Isaac's other slaves were to be citizens of a new nation.

Then, as the sail filled, the boom swung around with a crack, and we were darting forward at last. On the Manhattan landing, by lantern light, we could see people waiting. Over the roar of the storm, we heard them cheering us on. But Isaac's boat was sinking. The rope was tearing the mast out of the bottom. With a terrible crash, the mast broke and was carried over the side. A second later the bow smashed into the side of a wharf, and I found myself in the water swimming with one arm, clinging to Sana with the other.

My only hope was to let the shore current carry me out into midstream, and then, as the wind and tide thrust the boat toward the other shore, raise the sail and race for the Manhattan landing.

Fighting the rudder, I heard Sana's voice in my ear. "Will we make it, Samuel?" Water crashed over the side. Sana was bailing as fast as she could. "I can't swim, Samuel!" she cried into the wind. We were halfway across to Manhattan, and the boat was filling with sea. The gale was spinning us around. The rope was pulling us backward. I heaved at the sail, praying the mending wouldn't tear.

On the night that General Washington's army left Brooklyn, the worst storm I'd ever seen blew in from the Northeast. The wind howled. It drove the rain, stinging, into our eyes. It shook buildings and knocked down chimneys. And it whipped the water at Brooklyn Ferry into a sea of foam.

Down from the Heights in file marched Washington's army. The men entered the boats Major Gist and others had gathered at the ferry landing.

"What we need is a rope to cling to," someone said in the dark. "A rope stretching from here to Manhattan to guide us against the wind and current."

"There's rope here in the shipyard," a soldier remembered. "Buoys to float the rope across, too. But who can cross this flood in the dark?"

"Can you do it, Samuel?" Major Gist asked. "Can you get across with the rope?"

"I can do it, Major," I shouted, the wind tearing the words out of my mouth. But I wasn't sure. Even if the rope were fed out from shore slowly, the sail might split or the rope might tear down the mast. But the British ships were sure to force their way between Brooklyn and Manhattan. I had to try.

When the rope was ready, I tied it to the foot of the mast. Sana jumped into the boat. I shouted at her to stay behind, but she wouldn't move. There was no time to lose. I shoved off into the swirling current.

The next day the heavy rains continued. I spread the sail over the boat and slept snug and dry. Then I heard the voice I missed more than any in the world calling, "Samuel, Samuel Abraham!" Sana had found me! It was not a dream. "You chose, Samuel," she said. "You did it right. You chose our new country." From under her cloak she took a hot, steaming loaf wrapped in a napkin—her freedom bread, the sweetest I ever tasted. While we ate, she told me that Toby and Nathaniel were safe.

But this new country was in danger. Major Gist came to me again and explained that every boat was needed to carry Washington's army from Brooklyn to Manhattan. The army had to retreat that night. I was going to help save the army with Farmer Isaac's boat. Wouldn't he be surprised?

When I tied the boat to the dock below the Heights, Major Gist clapped his hands on my shoulders and looked me in the eyes. "Samuel," he said, "out in that creek you did more than many a free man for your country. I'd take it as a privilege if you'd consent to be my orderly and march beside me. And General Washington may need handy boatmen like you soon enough."

The next day it rained and rained. A thick sea fog covered the land. I looked everywhere for Sana. Many soldiers crowded into the camp, but they could tell me nothing. Alone and frightened, I mended the holes in my sail, pushing the big needle through the canvas, drawing it back again. Then, I heard voices nearby.

Major Gist stood there with an officer in a fine blue uniform. They asked me how deep the water was at this point between Brooklyn and Manhattan. They wanted to know if a British ship could sail between the two places. I told them that most ships could. Only the fog was keeping the British men-of-war from trapping Washington's army on Long Island.

The officer in the blue uniform thanked me. He and Major Gist walked away, looking thoughtful.

Just as I was raising the sail to race out of the creek, I glimpsed a big man in a blue coat and three-cornered hat alone in the bullreeds. He threw himself into the boat and ordered me to sail for Washington's camp. The British were close behind him. As we fled down the creek into New York Harbor, they fired at us from the banks. When the big man had caught his breath, he pointed up at the sail. Black holes gaped in the canvas.

"Musket balls," he said and winked. "Compliments of General Cornwallis."

As the boat carried us out into the harbor, I steered northward along the Brooklyn shore toward Brooklyn Heights and Washington's camp. I wondered what Farmer Isaac would say about his torn sail. But most of all, I wondered what had happened to Sana and Toby.

My passenger's name was Major Mordecai Gist. He commanded the Maryland soldiers who had held back the British while other Americans escaped. "Oh, what brave boys I lost today," said Major Gist, "and this war has only begun." He asked how I came to be fishing men out of the creek. I told him about Farmer Isaac, Sana, and Nathaniel.

As I pulled near, wet and weary men flopped into the boat. Others clung to the sides. "Row, row!" they shouted. I pulled on the oars with all my might. Out we shot into the current. Bullets splashed in the water near us. When we reached the far bank, the men cheered. I turned again into the creek and rowed back for more.

Six times I crossed the creek. Each time the battle grew closer, the fleeing Americans fewer. By now muddy water slopped around my ankles. My back ached from pulling on the oars.

I ran to the creek, pushed the boat out into the rushing tide, and slid the oars into their locks. On the opposite bank Americans were wading in the muddy water up to their waists, shouting for help. In the distance others were holding the British back from the water's edge. Great clouds of gunsmoke rolled over these brave soldiers. When the air cleared, I could see fewer and fewer of them.

Sana's eyes pleaded with me. She knew I tied my boat in the reeds along the creek. Her look said, "It's up to you, Samuel."

Nathaniel groaned. The small red spot on his bandage had begun to spread. Toby had come and was kneeling beside Sana. He shrugged. "You got the boat, Samuel. It's your choice."

Sana and Toby got set to carry Nathaniel up the road into the American lines. Sana caught me looking at the bag on her shoulder.

"That's my freedom flour," she said. "I'm going where I can bake my freedom loaf." A moment later, more soldiers ran between us. When they had passed, Sana, Toby, and Nathaniel were gone.

All at once the road was empty. From away in the distance came the roar of muskets. Isaac van Ditmas was gone. Sana was gone and the soldiers were, too. I was alone.

Was this freedom? I thought about that boy Nathaniel from far away. How a lot more people just like him were trapped in the marshes along the creek. And how Isaac sneered at them, and how the British king from across the waters sent his soldiers to shoot and imprison them. I looked at my hands, grown strong from pulling ropes and oars and sacks. Then I knew my choice. Those hands now were going to pull people, pull them to freedom.

"Stop staring," Sana shouted at me. "He's trembling. Wrap him in them empty sacks." Nathaniel told us how he swam across Gowanus Creek to escape from the British. But the tide was rising fast. Dozens of Americans were wounded and many couldn't swim. The army was trapped without boats in the swamps around the creek. Some were still fighting, but lots of soldiers were being shot like ducks in the marshes. Washington's men needed help badly.

Suddenly there was shouting. A soldier appeared in the doorway.
"The British are coming!" he cried. "The Americans are running!"

The road filled with crowds of American soldiers, now running
north along the road, back toward Washington's lines. Tired,
frightened people. Most were sopping wet. Where they stopped to
rest, the dust turned to mud under their feet.

Cannonballs were whizzing through the air. One crashed
through the roof of the mill. Farmer Isaac was nowhere to be seen.
Sana knelt by someone who had fallen beside the road. She tied a
strip of petticoat around a bloody gash in his leg. He was soaked
and shaking. When I looked at his face, I saw that he was
Nathaniel, the boy with the empty canteen.

When the officer was gone, and Isaac, too, one of his men stopped by the wagon. He just stood there and stared at me.

"You thirsty?" I asked him. He nodded and held his empty canteen upside down. I snatched my jug of buttermilk out of the wagon and poured it into the canteen. The boy took a long drink.

"Thanks," he said. "My name's Nathaniel. Joined up at Boston on my fourteenth birthday."

"You know how to shoot that thing?" I asked, pointing at his musket.

"Think so," he muttered. "Shot it yesterday in camp."

"You scared?" I asked him.

"No, I ain't," he said.

"Well, you oughta be," I told him.

All day long the guns crashed and boomed on the Long Island hills. While the mill wheel rumbled and ground, soldiers rushed down the South Road.

The next day, while I loaded sacks into a wagon, I heard the sound of fifes and drums. Southwards, along the road past the mill, came a hundred of Washington's recruits, their feet shuffling in the dust. An American officer rode beside them on a gray farmhorse.

"Captain!" Sana called to him. "Thousands of them are landing down the shore!"

"We know that, girl," he called back. "Don't worry, we'll handle them lobster backs. General Washington himself is coming over to Brooklyn." But the men marching past us didn't look so sure. Many seemed frightened. Some were barefoot. Some looked hungry and sick. Their flags drooped. As they passed, Sana read the names of the colonies embroidered on their banners: Pennsylvania, Delaware, Maryland, Rhode Island. They had come from far away to a strange place.

Farmer Isaac stood by the fence, puffing on his pipe. "You be quiet, girl. This isn't no fight of yours. If them fools want to break the king's law, they can get themselves killed with no help from my slaves."

Sana shook her head. I knew she felt sorry for the ragged men and boys marching past. Maybe they were not fighting for her liberty. Not yet. But freedom had to start somewhere. That summer it was starting in Brooklyn.

Back in the kitchen of the big house, I told what I had seen.

"Those great ships have hundreds of cannon," Toby said.

"There's got to be thousands of Redcoats," somebody else said, "and they gonna whip these Liberty Boys but good."

"General Washington will find a way," Sana said, but her eyes held back tears. "It can't just end like this!"

Old Toby put an arm around her. "Trouble is, dear, it can. These Americans are settin' up to fight their king, and that means all the king's ships, and men, and cannon."

"No business for us black slaves, I'm tellin' you," said Joseph Martin.

"Not with Isaac down so hard on the Liberty Boys," Loretta added.

It seemed to me the slaves were right. I could not think how the ordinary Americans I had seen, fresh from their farms and shops, could ever drive away an army of real soldiers.

So the summer of 1776, my fourteenth one, passed on. Day by day, my back and arms grew stronger with hard work. More than once I looked up from filling flour sacks to find a cool jar of buttermilk left by Sana. Then I'd drink the milk and fill the empty jar with flour. When she fetched the jar back, she would hide it. One day I asked what she wanted with so much flour. She just smiled and said, "That flour will be bread for our freedom day."

While I sailed on Farmer Isaac's errands or loaded sacks of flour, the war crept towards Brooklyn. On a fine morning we woke in the slave quarters to the thunder of great guns out in the harbor. I ran up to the house. Sana just kept on calmly with her work. "Washington's come to New York," she said, grinning. "Those are guns out of Governors Island practicing to scare off the British."

Well, the guns sure scared off Farmer Isaac. After Washington arrived, he and Mrs. van Ditmas never crossed to Manhattan again. I hoisted the sail of my boat to carry the farmer's wife and daughters, with all their trunks, to an old uncle's house on Staten Island.

And there on Staten Island, I saw them. The king's army had come from across the sea and on the hillside meadows had pitched its tents by the thousands. The sun glinted on rows of brass cannon and bayonets. Redcoats came down from the hills. They spread over the green grass like streams of blood, and they sat in barges and were rowed across to the Brooklyn shore. A barge passed nearby. We saw the smiling, sunburned faces of the soldiers. "Hurrah!" they cheered, and the van Ditmas girls waved and giggled.

When the Sons of Liberty finally came, waving their flags, Isaac locked us in the house.

In the kitchen, the servants argued. "Liberty ain't for Africans," one said. "And it got nothin' to do with us," another said.

But Sana just shook her head. She was fifteen and had been to church school. She could write her name and could read. "Nobody here's gonna be free unless they take the risk. Open your eyes! War is coming to Brooklyn 'tween that English king and those Sons of Liberty. We can't say who'll win. We can't say how many black slaves are ever gonna get free. But one thing is sure—it's never gonna happen under Isaac van Ditmas."

The talk made my head spin. One moment it seemed to offer hope, and then the arguments turned and I didn't feel hope anymore. One day Liberty men nailed a proclamation to a tree by the South Road. But before anyone could tell me what it said, Isaac came and tore it down and stamped on it in the dust. That was the day Sana promised she would teach me to read. "That writing, Samuel," she said later, "was the Declaration of Independence, made by Thomas Jefferson in the Congress at Philadelphia."

"How they get free, Toby?"

"Why they up and said they was free, girl, and wrote those words down on paper."

Sana laughed. "You gotta do more than say you're free. That king and Isaac, do they care what anybody say?"

What was it, I wondered, that made people think they could change their lives? They called their freedom "liberty," and they marched through Brooklyn town cheering for that liberty.

America, being ruled by the king of England, was not a separate country. And these were troubled times in all the colonies. The night came when Manhattan Island was lit up like daytime with a hundred bonfires. We gathered on the steps of the great house and heard the cheers and shouts echo over the water. Then came the sound of drums and fifes, songs and cannon firing.

"What's all that racket over there?" Sana asked.

"That's the sound of people going free," old Toby answered. "Free from the king of England. Free from the likes of van Ditmas."

When Farmer Isaac saw that I had grown strong and could row a boat well, he taught me about the currents that flow between Brooklyn and Manhattan, about setting a sail and holding a course. I was to row Mrs. van Ditmas and her daughters over to Manhattan, or down the Brooklyn shore to Staten Island across the harbor. Isaac shook me by the collar and warned me never to row or sail except where he sent me. I was his property, according to the laws of the Crown Colony, and he could do what he wanted with me.

Work you do not choose to do is always tiring. And even the house slaves, who labored in Farmer Isaac's kitchen, got little sleep and less food. Whenever I felt the fresh sea breeze on my face, I would look up at the gulls flying where they pleased and I would dream. I wondered how it was to be free like them, to go where I wanted.

Gowanus Creek, where the flour mill stood, wound out of this harbor into the green fields and lost itself in ponds and marshes. On a summer evening, the mosquitoes rose like clouds from still waters and settled, stinging, on our bare arms and necks.

Farmer Isaac was a strict man. Our day began at sunrise and ended when the light faded. Round and round the great stone wheel rolled and rumbled all day long, driven by tides flowing in and out of the creek. We ground wheat to make bread at the mill. We shoveled the flour into bags, and loaded the bags into boats, to be brought to bakers in Manhattan. But little bread we ever saw. Van Ditmas was a stingy man. Many nights I went to bed with my stomach growling and only the taste of the raw flour on my lips.

My MASTER, ISAAC VAN DITMAS, was a very rich farmer. In my fourteenth year, he bought me from his old aunt in Flushing and took me from my parents to work as a slave in his flour mill on Gowanus Creek in Brooklyn. That same time he bought Sana Williams, Toby, and others to keep the gardens and kitchen of his big house on New York Harbor.

At the end of Long Island, the Heights of Brooklyn overlooked the East River and Manhattan Island. To the south lay the town of Brooklyn; it was only a small one in those days. The long South Road ran across Long Island's hills, through fields of wheat and rye, connecting Brooklyn town with the Narrows at the entrance to New York Harbor.

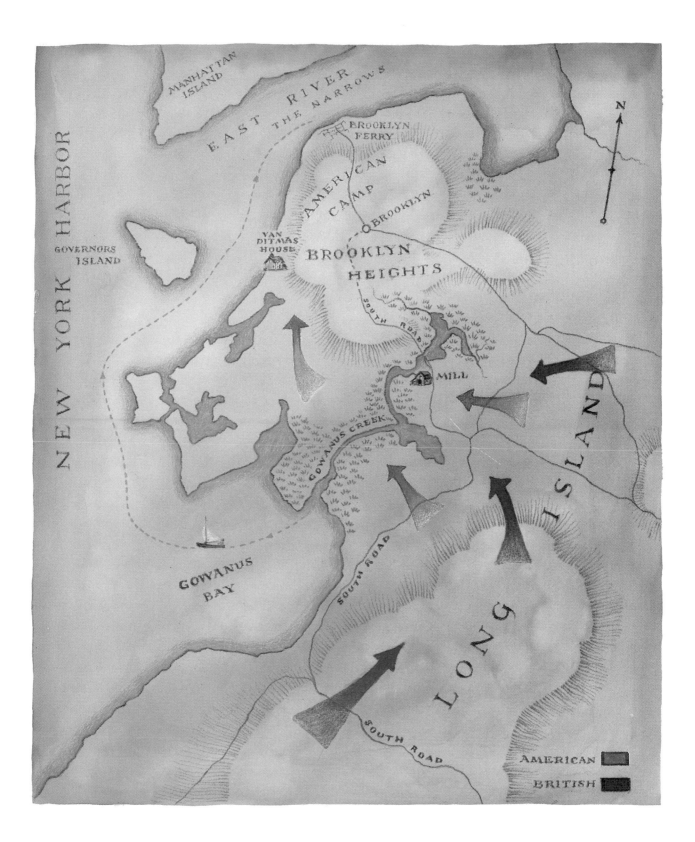

FOR HANNA. R.B.
FOR DŌ. J.W.

Library of Congress Cataloging-in-Publication Data

Berleth, Richard J.
Samuel's choice/Richard Berleth;
illustrated by James Watling.

p. cm.

Summary: Samuel, a fourteen-year-old slave in Brooklyn
in 1776, faces a difficult choice when the fighting
between the British and the colonists reaches his
doorstep and only he can help the rebels.
ISBN 0-8075-7218-7
1. Long Island, Battle of, 1776—Juvenile fiction.
[1. Long Island, Battle of, 1776—Fiction. 2. United
States—History—Revolution, 1775-1783—Campaigns—
Fiction. 3. Afro-Americans—Fiction.] I. Watling,
James, ill. II. Title.
PZ7.B4533Sam 1990   89-77186
[Fic]—dc20   CIP
                                               AC

Text © 1990 by Richard J. Berleth.
Illustrations © 1990 by James Watling.
Design by Karen Johnson Campbell.
Published in 1990 by Albert Whitman & Company,
6340 Oakton Street, Morton Grove, Illinois 60053.
Published simultaneously in Canada by
General Publishing, Limited, Toronto.
Printed in the United States of America.
10   9   8   7   6   5

The text is set in Garamond No. 3.
The illustrations are colored ink and colored pencil.

Samuel's Choice

RICHARD BERLETH

illustrated by JAMES WATLING

ALBERT WHITMAN & COMPANY, MORTON GROVE, ILLINOIS